# NOW IN FULL COLOUR

# CAPTAIN UNDERPANTS

## AND THE INVASION OF THE Incredibly Naughty Cafeteria Ladies From Outer Space (and the Subsequent Assault of The Equally Evil Lunchroom Zombie Nerds)

The Third Epic Novel by

# DAV PILKEY

with colour by Jose Garibaldi

**SCHOLASTIC**

Scholastic Children's Books
An imprint of Scholastic Ltd
Euston House, 24 Eversholt Street
London, NW1 1DB, UK
Registered office: Westfield Road, Southam, Warwickshire, CV47 0RA
SCHOLASTIC and associated logos are trademarks and/or registered
trademarks of Scholastic Inc.

First published in the US by Scholastic Inc, 1999
First published in the UK by Scholastic Ltd, 2000

This edition published by Scholastic Ltd, 2014

Trade ISBN 978 1407 15824 2
Non Trade ISBN 978 1407 15840 2

A CIP catalogue record for this book is available from the
British Library.

Printed and bound in Italy
Papers used by Scholastic Children's Books are made from wood grown
in sustainable forests.

1 3 5 7 9 10 8 6 4 2

www.scholastic.co.uk

Be sure to check out
Dav Pilkey's Extra-Crunchy Web Site O' Fun at
www.pilkey.com

For John "Sparky" Johnson

# CHAPTERS

George Beard and
Harold Hutchins
present:
A "Deny Everything"
Production

CAPTAIN
WEDGIE
WARS
UNDERPANTS

**EPISODE 1**

The Fantom
Principal

A Long time Ago, in a
Elementary School far
far away...

There were two
cool kids Named
George and Harold.

WE
rule

ME
TOO

They had a evil
Principle Named
Mr. Krupp, who was
Strong in
The ways
of The
FORSE!

Blah
Blah

He FORSED
Them to Study

Blah Blah Blah

He FORSED
Them to Clean

BLAH
BLAH
BLAH

And he forsed
Them To
BEHAVE!

HA HA
HA!

So George and Harold Hipnotised Him.

You will obey our every command!

"SNAP!

OK.

You Are Now "Captain Underpants"

OK

HA HA HA

It started out as A Joke, but it WASENT Funny for Long!

HA HA HA

Tra-La-Laaa

Hey

Come Back

Mr. Krupp Thougt He really was The Worlds greatest Super-hero. He got into All Kinds of Trouble.

George and Harold had to Save him (and the entire planet)...

...Twice!

Now The only way they can Turn Captain Under-Pants back into MR. Krupp, is to pour water over his head!

But The worst Part is That George and Harold Have To Keep An eye on mr. Krupp.

Blah Blah Blah

Because for some **STRANGE** reason, whenever he hears sombody snap There fingers...

SNAP!

... he Turns BACK into you-know-who!

TRA LA LAAA

So whatever you Do, **PLEASE DON'T** snap your fingers Around Mr. Krupp.

You heard the man! **PLEASE PLEASE, PLEASE** Don't SNAP Those Fingers!

This has been A public servise Anouncement from George and Harold... who **STILL** Deny everything!

# CHAPTER 1
## GEORGE AND HAROLD

This is George Beard and Harold Hutchins.
George is the kid on the left with the tie
and the flat-top. Harold is the one on the
right with the T-shirt and the bad haircut.
Remember that now.

If you were looking for a few words to describe George and Harold, you might come up with *kind*, *funny*, *smart*, *determined* and *deep*.

Just ask their principal, Mr Krupp. He'll tell you that George and Harold are **KIND**a **FUNNY**-lookin' **SMART** alecks who are **DETERMINED** to drive everybody off the **DEEP** end!

But don't listen to him.

George and Harold are actually very clever and good-hearted boys. Their only problem is that they're fourth graders. And at George and Harold's school, fourth graders are expected to sit still and pay attention for *seven hours a day*!

George and Harold are just not very good at that.

The only thing George and Harold *are* good at is being silly. Unfortunately, George and Harold's silliness gets them into trouble every now and then. Sometimes it gets them into a LOT of trouble. And one time it got them into *SO MUCH* trouble, it almost caused the entire Earth to be destroyed by an army of giant evil zombie nerds!

But before I can tell you that story, I have to tell you *this* story. . .

## CHAPTER 2
# THE EVIL SPACE GUYS

One dark, clear night in Piqua, Ohio, a flaming object was seen streaking across the quiet midnight sky.

It shone brightly for a second or two, then fizzled out just above Jerome Horwitz Elementary School. Nobody gave it a second thought.

The next day, everything seemed pretty normal. Nobody noticed anything different about the school. Nobody paid any attention to the roof. And of course, nobody looked up and said, "Hey, what's that big spaceship thingy doing on the roof of the school?"

Perhaps if they had, the horrible ordeal that followed might never have happened, and you wouldn't be sitting here reading about it right now. But they didn't, it did, and, well, here we are.

As we can all plainly see, there was a spaceship on top of the building. And inside that spaceship were three of the most evil, hideous and merciless spacemen ever to set foot on the roof of a small midwestern elementary school.

Their names were Zorx, Klax and Jennifer. Their mission? To take over planet Earth.

"First," said Zorx, "we must find a way to infiltrate the school."

"Then," said Klax, "we will turn all the children into giant, super-powered evil zombie nerds!"

"Finally," said Jennifer, "we will use them to take over the world!" Zorx and Klax laughed and laughed.

*"Silence, you fools!"* barked Jennifer. "If our plan is to work, we must wait until it is narratively convenient. In the meantime, we will watch their every move on our trinocloscope!"

# CHAPTER 3
# FUN WITH SCIENCE

Early that same morning, George and Harold were sitting in their 10:15 A.M. science class making silly noises.

"Meeowwwww," George mewed softly, without moving his lips.

"Rrrr-rrr-rrrr," growled Harold, without opening his mouth.

"There it is *again*!" exclaimed their science teacher, Mr Fyde. "I *distinctly* heard a cat and a dog in here!"

"We didn't hear anything," the children said, trying not to laugh.

"I-I must be *hearing* things again," Mr Fyde worried.

"Maybe you should leave and go see a doctor," said George with concern.

"I can't," said Mr Fyde. "Today is the day of the big *volcano experiment*."

The children all groaned. Mr Fyde's science experiments were usually the most idiotic things on earth. They almost never worked, and were *always* boring.

But today's experiment was different. Mr Fyde brought in a large, fake-looking volcano that he had made out of papier-mâché. He filled the volcano with a box of ordinary baking soda.

"Baking soda is also called 'sodium bicarbonate'," explained Mr Fyde.

"Meeeeowwwwwww."

"Umm. . ." said Mr Fyde, "did any of you children just hear – umm, uh . . . never mind."

Mr Fyde opened up a bottle of clear liquid. "Now watch what happens when I pour vinegar into the baking soda," he said.

The children watched as the tiny volcano started to rumble. Soon, a large glob of foamy goop spurted out the top. The goop poured over the desk and dripped on to the floor, creating a huge mess.

"Oops," said Mr Fyde. "I guess I used too much baking soda."

George and Harold were stunned.

"How did you do that?" asked Harold.

"Well," said Mr Fyde, "the vinegar acts as a liberating agent, which releases the gaseous carbonate radical element of the sodium bicarbo—"

"Meeeeooowwwwwwww."

"Umm . . . uh," Mr Fyde paused. "Uh, e-excuse me, children. I-I've got to go and see a doctor."

Mr Fyde put on his coat and hurried
out the door. George and Harold got up
and studied the messy volcano experiment
with great interest.

"Are you thinking what I'm thinking?"
asked George.

"I think I'm thinking what you're
thinking," said Harold.

# CHAPTER 4
# THE SET-UP

After school, the two boys raced to
George's house and got down to business.

George and Harold sat down and began creating a fake cupcake recipe.

"We'll just add a box of baking soda and a bottle of vinegar to this recipe," said George. "And whoever makes these cupcakes will get a big surprise!"

"Let's add *two* boxes of baking soda and *two* bottles of vinegar to the recipe," said Harold. "That way, they'll get an even *bigger* surprise!"

"Good idea!" laughed George.

# CHAPTER 5
# MR KRUPP'S KRISPY KRUPCAKES

The next morning at school, George and Harold strolled into the cafeteria and taped a festive-looking card to the kitchen door.

Soon the lunch ladies arrived.

"Oh, look," said Miss Creant, the head lunch lady. "Today is Mr Krupp's birthday and he'd like us to make a batch of cupcakes just for him! Isn't that cute?"

"I've got an idea," said the cook, Mrs DePoint. "Why don't we surprise him and make cupcakes for the *whole school*!"

"Good thinking," said Miss Creant. "Let's see now . . . this recipe serves ten, and we have about 1,000 students and faculty in the school, so. . .

. . .we'll need 100 eggs, 150 cups of flour, 200 boxes of baking soda, 7 quarts of green food colouring, 50 sticks of butter, 150 cups of sugar – and, let's see. . . Oh yes, 200 bottles of *vinegar*!"

# MR. KRUPP'S KRISPY KRUPCAKES

### INGREDIENTS

1 egg
1½ cups of Flour
2 Boxes BAKing Soda
1½ Cups SugAR
½ Stick Butter
Green Food coleRing
2 Bottles VinegAr

MAkes 10 CupCAkes

### DiRections

Mix FLour And SugAr with baking Soda, and egg. Melt butter, pour into Mixture. Stir in Food coleRing. Now Add VinegAr. Mix well. Pour into CupcAke Thingies. BAke At 45 degrees For 3 hours.

The lunch ladies scurried about, gathering everything they needed. They dumped the eggs, food colouring, milk and baking soda into a large vat and began to mix thoroughly.

Then somebody poured in the vinegar. . .

# CHAPTER 6
## WHAT HAPPENED NEXT

(Note: Please shake this book back and forth uncontrollably when you read the following word. Also, shout it out as loud as you can. Don't worry, you won't get in trouble.)

### "KA-BLOOOOOSH!"

# CHAPTER 6½
## HERE COMES THE GOOP!

A giant wave of green goop crashed through the cafeteria doors and splashed down the halls, swallowing everything in its path. Book bags, bulletin boards, lunch boxes, coat racks, trophy cases . . . nothing could stand in the way of the gigantic green glob o' goo.

It traveled down the north, east and west wings of the school, covering everything from the drinking fountains to the text on this page. It squished into lockers, and squashed down the stairs. It bille~~~ int~~~ ~~~ and ballo~~~

It wasn't long before the green goop
began spilling into all the classrooms.

"Uh-oh," said George. "Something tells
me the lunch ladies made more than just
*one* batch of Mr Krupp's Krispy Krupcakes."

"But-but that was *their* idea, not
*ours*," cried Harold.

"Speaking of *ideas*," said George, "I've
got a good one."

"What?" asked Harold.

*"RUN!"* cried George.

# CHAPTER 7
# THE WRATH OF THE CAFETERIA LADIES

The next afternoon, as cleaning crews sorted through the sticky green hallways and sticky green classrooms, the cafeteria ladies had a meeting with Mr Krupp in his sticky green office.

*"But it wasn't even my birthday!"* cried Mr Krupp.

"We know you had nothing to do with this!" said Miss Creant. "We think it was those two awful boys, George and Harold!"

"Well, *duh!*" said Mr Krupp, rolling his eyes. "OF COURSE IT WAS GEORGE AND HAROLD!!! But do you have any proof?"

"PROOF?!!?" said the lunch ladies. "Why, George and Harold are *always* playing tricks on us! Every day, they change the letters around on our lunch sign. They put pepper in the napkin dispensers and unscrew the caps on the saltshakers. . . They start food fights. . . They go sledging on our lunch trays. . . They make everybody laugh so the milk squirts out their noses. . . And they're *constantly creating these awful comic books about us*!!!"

# CHAPTER 8
# CAPTAIN UNDERPANTS AND THE NIGHT OF THE LIVING LUNCH LADIES

By George Beard
and Harold Hutchins.

# CAPTain UNderpants and the NIGHT of THE Living LUNCH LADYS

## Story By George Beard
## Pictures By Harold Hutchins

Late one friday Afternoon, The Lunch Ladys were Cleaning up The CAFFeteria.

There's Lots of half-eaten Food in This TRASH Barrel.

Well Pour it in and we'll Serve it agAin next WEEK!

TRASH

STEW

WASTE not waNt Not!

TRASH

STEW

But while they were Working, The janiter AXidentALLy locked The school for The weekend.

♪

Closed

The Lunch Ladys were TRAPPed inside!

HELP!

They were Forsed to eat There own Food To Survive.

Past The Lips

Andover The gums..

Look out Tummy... Here it Comes.

When The Janiter returned on monday morning, The Lunch Ladies were dead... Victims of Their own cooking.

Oopsy Daisys

The janiter Took the dead Lunch Ladys up the hill to bury Them.

Hmmm... That Looks like a good Place.

BURY DEAD STUFF Here

But it wasn't!

WARNING: THIS HiLL IS HAUNTED! WHATever you DO, DON'T BURY DEAD STUFF Here

CRASH

RIP

RIP

RIP

THEY GOT into A BIG FIGHT.

Captain Under-pants WAS Faster Than a speeding WAIStbAnd...

...More Powerful Than Boxer Shorts...

.And Able to Leap tall buildings Without getting a wedgie.

TRA La LAAAA

But the Lunch Ladys were Strong Too. They RAn Faster Than Their Runny Meatloaf GRAVY.

They were more Powerful Than The Stench of Their "sloppy-Joe" CassAroLe

ANd they could Leap Tall Buildings With The gassy After-Affects of Their "Texas-style" Three-bean chili con Carney.

B-R-R-R-R-T

Soon they were ALL on top of A tall building.

We've got you Now, Waistband Warrior!

NOT SO FAST!

Captain Underpants Pressed A button on his "Utility Waistband"
Click

And out popped A Roll of Toilet Paper.

Even The living Dead can't exscape the "Toilet Paper of Justice."

Captain Underpants Lassoed the Lecherous Lunch Ladies.

But they had A trick up there sleeves.
Lunch Lady Brand SALSBURY STEAK SAUCE

They poured the steak sauce on the toilet paper of Justice.
sssss

# CHAPTER 9
## QUITTIN' TIME

"We're *fed up* with those two boys!" cried Miss Creant. "They're always making fun of our cooking!"

"Yeah!" said Mrs DePoint. "Our food isn't *that* bad. I ate here once and hardly got sick at all!"

"Well, I can't punish them if we don't have any proof," said Mr Krupp.

"Fine!" said the lunch ladies. "Then we *quit*!"

"Ladies, ladies," cried Mr Krupp. "Be reasonable! You can't just *quit* on such short notice."

But the lunch ladies didn't care. They marched right out of Mr Krupp's sticky green office, and that was the end of that.

"Rats!" cried Mr Krupp. "Now where am I going to find three new lunch ladies by tomorrow morning?"

Suddenly there was a knock on Mr Krupp's door. Three very large women wearing *lots* of make-up walked into his office.

"Hello," said the first woman. "My name is, uh, Zorx*ette*. These are my, uh, sisters, *Klaxette* and, umm, *Jenniferette*. We've come to apply for jobs as cafeteria ladies."

"Wow," said Mr Krupp. "Do you have any experience?"

"No," said Klaxette.

"Do you have any credentials?" asked Mr Krupp.

"No," said Zorxette.

"Do you have any references?" asked Mr Krupp.

"No," said Jenniferette.

"You're hired!" said Mr Krupp.

"Wonderful," said Jenniferette. "Now our plan to take over the world is – er, I mean, our plan to *feed the children healthy, nutritional meals* is underway!"

The three new lunch ladies laughed horribly. Then they left Mr Krupp's office and got started preparing the next day's lunch menu.

"Well, *that* was easy," said Mr Krupp.
"Now to take care of George and Harold!"

# CHAPTER 10
## BUSTED!

George and Harold were in study hall when they heard the dreaded announcement over the intercom:

"**George Beard and Harold Hutchins, please report to Mr Krupp's office immediately.**"

"Oh, no," cried Harold. "We're busted!"
"No way!" said George. "Remember, what happened yesterday was *not our fault*! We didn't do it – it was an *accident*!"

But Mr Krupp was not as understanding. "I can't prove it, but I *know* you boys are responsible for yesterday's disaster," Mr Krupp said. "I'm going to punish you by taking away your cafeteria privileges for the rest of the year! *No more cafeteria food for you two!*"

"No more cafeteria food?" whispered Harold, "I thought he said he was going to *punish* us."

"Yeah." George smiled. "Maybe if we're *really* bad, he'll take away our *homework* privileges, too!"

*"I heard that!"* screamed Mr Krupp. "From now on, you boys are going to have to pack your own lunches and eat in my office so I can keep an eye on you!"

"Rats!" said Harold.

"But we didn't do it!" George protested. "WE DIDN'T DO IT!"

"Too bad, bub!" said Mr Krupp.

"Boy," said George. "This is probably the first time we've gotten in trouble for something we *didn't* do."

"Unless you count all those times we didn't do our homework," said Harold.

"Oh, yeah," laughed George.

# CHAPTER 11
## BROWN BAGGIN' IT

The next day, George and Harold each brought their own sandwiches to Mr Krupp's office for lunch.

"I'll trade you half of my peanut-butter-and-gummy-worm sandwich," said George, "for half of your tuna-salad-with-chocolate-chips-and-miniature-marshmallows sandwich."

"Sure," said Harold. "Y'want some barbecue sauce on that?"

"You kids are DISGUSTING!" Mr Krupp shouted.

Soon George and Harold were munching on potato chips with whipped cream and chocolate sprinkles. Mr Krupp was turning green.

"What's for dessert?" asked Harold.

"Hard-boiled eggs dipped in hot fudge and Skittles!" said George.

"AAAUGH!" screamed Mr Krupp. *"I can't stand it any more!"* He got up and stumbled out the door for some fresh air.

"You know," said George. "Now that Mr Krupp is gone, we could run to the cafeteria and change the letters around on the lunch sign."

"Cool," said Harold.

So George and Harold sneaked to the
cafeteria. But when they read the lunch
sign, they were a bit confused.

"What's going on here?" said George.

"It looks like somebody's already
changed the sign," said Harold.

"Forget the sign," said George. "Look
at everybody! *They've* changed!"

57

It was true. All the kids and teachers in school were entering the cafeteria looking as normal as ever. But they were leaving the cafeteria looking quite different.

"Look!" cried George. "They're all wearing broken eyeglasses held together with masking tape . . . and they've all got vinyl pocket protectors!!! They've all turned into—"

"*Nerds!*" Harold gasped.

"And look at their skin," said George. "They're all grey and clammy. That could only mean one thing!"

"They're – they're ZOMBIE nerds?!!?" asked Harold.

"I'm afraid so," said George.

"Let's just hope they're friendly!" said Harold.

"Whoever heard of a *friendly* zombie nerd?" asked George.

"I'm afraid," Harold whined.

"There's no time to be afraid," said George. "We've got to get to the bottom of this!"

"*That's* what I'm afraid of," said Harold.

# CHAPTER 12
## THE BOTTOM OF THIS

George and Harold crawled into the cafeteria and sneaked through the kitchen doors. There they hid behind a table while the incredibly naughty cafeteria ladies from outer space discussed their plans to take over the world.

"Look at those puny earthlings!" laughed Zorx. "They're all drinking EVIL ZOMBIE NERD MILKSHAKES and transforming before our very eyes!"

"It won't be long now," said Klax. "Tomorrow, we'll feed them SUPER EVIL RAPID-GROWTH JUICE! Then they will grow to the size of Xleqxisfp trees."

"Exactly," sneered Jennifer. "Then we will unleash our giant evil zombie nerds upon the earth, and soon the planet will be OURS!"

The three evil space guys threw back their heads and laughed hysterically.

"We've got to tell Mr Krupp about this,"
Harold whispered.

"Right," whispered George. "But first,
we've got to get rid of that SUPER EVIL
RAPID-GROWTH JUICE!

George carefully reached up and swiped
the carton of juice.

"What should we do with it?" asked
Harold.

"Let's pour it out the window," said
George. "That way it won't do any damage."

"Good idea," said Harold.

63

While the naughty cafeteria ladies continued laughing, George quietly emptied the carton of SUPER EVIL RAPID-GROWTH JUICE out the window.

"You know," whispered Harold, "Mr Krupp is never going to believe that sinister cafeteria ladies from outer space have turned everybody into evil zombie nerds."

"Sure he'll believe us – he's **GOT** to believe us!" said George. ". . .I *hope* he believes us!"

# CHAPTER 13
## HE DOESN'T
## BELIEVE THEM

"That's the most *ridiculous* story I've ever heard!" laughed Mr Krupp.

"But it's true!" cried Harold.

"Yeah," said George. "Everybody in the entire school is an evil zombie nerd! The kids, the teachers . . . *everybody*!"

"All right," said Mr Krupp. "I'll prove it to you!" He pressed the button on his intercom and called for his secretary.

Soon Miss Anthrope entered the room. She was dressed in a pink polka-dot polyester dress, with orthopedic knee-high stockings and ugly brown arch-support loafers.

"*See?*" said Harold. "She's dressed like a *nerd*!"

"*She always dresses like that,*" snapped Mr Krupp.

"But she's grey and clammy and reeks of *freakish zombified death*!" cried George.

"She *always smells like that*!" Mr Krupp argued. "And she's always grey and clammy, too!"

George and Harold had to admit that school secretaries were not very good subjects to compare and contrast with evil zombie nerds.

But then, Miss Anthrope leaned over and took a huge bite out of Mr Krupp's desk. *"Must destroy Earth,"* she moaned as she took another bite.

Even Mr Krupp had to agree that Miss Anthrope was acting a bit more evil than usual.

So George and Harold took Mr Krupp down to the cafeteria to confront the evil lunch ladies.

Suddenly, out of the shadows stepped the evil Zorx. "Gotcha!" Zorx cried, as he grabbed onto Harold's shoulders.

"Aaaagh!" screamed Harold. He squirmed away, pulling Zorx's gloves off and revealing two slimy green tentacles.

"See, Mr Krupp?" said George. "We told you they were space guys!"

"*You FOOLS!*" screamed Zorx. "Now we
will destroy you!" The evil Zorx pointed
his tentacle at George, Harold and Mr
Krupp, and snapped his fingers:

*SNAP!*

Suddenly, Mr Krupp began to change.

A heroic grin spread across Mr Krupp's
face. He threw out his chest and placed
his fists firmly at his sides, looking quite
triumphant.

"Uh-oh," said George. "That evil space
guy just snapped his fingers! Now Mr
Krupp is turning into *you-know-who*!"

"Hey, wait a second," said Harold.
"Tentacles don't have fingers! You can't
*snap* a tentacle!"

"There's no time to argue the physical
improbabilities of this story," said George.
"We've got to stop Mr Krupp from
changing into Captain Underpants before
it's too late!"

# CHAPTER 14
## IT'S TOO LATE

Mr Krupp turned and dashed out the door. His clothes flew off behind him as the hallways echoed with jubilant proclamations about the superiority of underwear.

George and Harold dashed after him, but the door was quickly blocked by Zorx, Klax and Jennifer.

"You wanna get out of this kitchen," the evil Jennifer mocked, "you gotta go through *US*!"

George grabbed a rolling pin. Harold grabbed a cast-iron frying pan.

"I sure hope we don't have to resort to incredibly graphic violence," said Harold.

"Me, too," said George.

# CHAPTER 15
# THE INCREDIBLY GRAPHIC VIOLENCE CHAPTER, PART 1 (IN FLIP-O-RAMA™)

# WARNING:

The following chapter contains terribly inappropriate scenes that certainly do not belong in a children's book.

If you are offended by such senselessness, please put this book down immediately, raise your arms over your head and run screaming to your nearest shoe store.

When you get there, ask them to make you a cheeseburger.

(Note: This probably won't help you a bit, but we think it will be funny.)

# PILKEY® BRAND

# O.RAMA

## HERE'S HOW IT WORKS!

### Step 1
Place your *left* hand inside the dotted lines marked "LEFT HAND HERE". Hold the book open *flat*.

### Step 2
Grasp the *right-hand* page with your right thumb and index finger (inside the dotted lines marked "RIGHT THUMB HERE").

### Step 3
Now *quickly* flip the right-hand page back and forth until the picture appears to be *animated*.

(For extra fun, try adding your own sound-effects!)

# FLIP-O-RAMA 1

(pages 77 and 79)

Remember, flip *only* page 77.
While you are flipping, be sure you
can see the picture on page 77
*and* the one on page 79.
If you flip quickly, the two
pictures will start to look like
<u>one</u> *animated* picture.

Don't forget to
add your own sound-effects!

LEFT HAND HERE

## GEORGE PINS
## A PREDATOR.

77

RIGHT
THUMB
HERE

**GEORGE PINS
A PREDATOR.**

# FLIP-O-RAMA 2

(pages 81 and 83)

Remember, flip *only* page 81.
While you are flipping, be sure you
can see the picture on page 81
*and* the one on page 83.
If you flip quickly, the two
pictures will start to look like
<u>one</u> *animated* picture.

Don't forget to
add your own sound-effects!

LEFT HAND HERE

# HAROLD BONKS
# A BAD GUY.

RIGHT
THUMB
HERE

82

**HAROLD BONKS
A BAD GUY.**

# FLIP-O-RAMA 3

(pages 85 and 87)

Remember, flip *only* page 85.
While you are flipping, be sure you
can see the picture on page 85
*and* the one on page 87.
If you flip quickly, the two
pictures will start to look like
<u>one</u> *animated* picture.

Don't forget to
add your own sound-effects!

LEFT HAND HERE

GEORGE AND HAROLD
SAVE THE DAY!
(FOR NOW)

RIGHT
THUMB
HERE

GEORGE AND HAROLD
SAVE THE DAY!
(FOR NOW)

# CHAPTER 16
## THE ASSAULT OF THE EQUALLY EVIL LUNCHROOM ZOMBIE NERDS

George and Harold had barely caught their breath when Captain Underpants finally showed up.

"Tra-La-Laaaaa!" he said. "I'm here to fight for Truth, Justice and *all* that is Pre-Shrunk and Cottony!"

"Where were you back in chapter fifteen when we needed you?" asked George.

"I was at the shoe store ordering a cheeseburger," said Captain Underpants.

While our three heroes were talking,
nobody noticed that Zorx, Klax and
Jennifer had slithered away. The wounded
space guys approached the lunchroom
loudspeakers and called for their evil
zombie nerds.

"Zombie nerds!" instructed Jennifer.
"Destroy Captain Underpants – and his
little friends, too!"

Soon, every evil zombie nerd in the
entire school put down their *Omni*
magazines and headed for the cafeteria.

"*Must destroy Underpants,*" they
groaned. "*Must destroy Underpants!*"

Suddenly, our three heroes were
surrounded by evil, vicious zombie
nerds. Closer and closer they came.

"Oh, no!" cried George. "What do we
do now?"

"To the Underwear Cave!" shouted
Captain Underpants.

"There *is* no *Underwear Cave*!" said
Harold.

"Really?" said Captain Underpants. "Well,
let's just climb up that ladder instead."

George, Harold and Captain
Underpants scurried up the ladder, and
soon they were all on the roof.

"Well, we're safe now," said Harold.

"Yep," said George.

"That's for sure," said Captain
Underpants.

# CHAPTER 17
## OH YEAH?

It didn't take long before George, Harold
and Captain Underpants looked behind
them.

"Hey," said Harold. "What's that big
spaceship thingy doing on the roof of the
school?"

"And where did that *super evil rapidly growing* dandelion come from?" asked Captain Underpants.

George and Harold gasped. They looked at each other with the sudden panicked realization that only children who have accidentally created a giant mutated garden nuisance would know.

"Er –" stammered George. "We have *no idea* how *that* happened."

"Er – *yeah*," said Harold. "Absolutely *no idea* at all!"

At that moment, the door to the roof swung open. Zorx poked his evil head out and shouted, "We've got you now!"

With no place else to run, our three heroes quickly scurried up the ladder of the big spaceship thingy and closed the door behind them.

Inside the spaceship, George, Harold and Captain Underpants discovered a refrigerator filled with strange juices.

"Look," said George. "Here's a carton of Anti-Evil Zombie Nerd Juice. How convenient!"

"And look at this," said Harold. "A carton of Ultra Nasty Self-Destruct Juice. Now *this* could come in handy!"

"And look what I've found," said Captain Underpants. "A whole carton of Extra-Strength Super Power Juice!"

"Hey, gimme that!" said George, snapping the carton out of Captain Underpants's hands.

# CHAPTER 18
## SPACE SLAVES

Suddenly, the door of the spaceship swung open, and the three evil space guys slithered inside.

"Step away from the refrigerator!" screamed Jennifer. "And get into that jail cell!"

George and Harold hid their juice cartons behind their backs, and our three heroes stepped quickly into the jail cell.

Zorx started up the engines and the
spaceship lifted off. It rose a hundred metres
in the air and hovered over the school.

"You three puny earthlings are very
fortunate," said Jennifer. "You will get to
witness the destruction of your planet
from the safety of your jail cell. Afterwards,
you will have the honour of being our
obedient space slaves!"

"Aw, *man!*" said George and Harold.

"Quickly, Klax," said Jennifer. "Get me
a carton of SUPER EVIL RAPID-GROWTH JUICE
from the refrigerator. We can pour it into
our spray gun and shower it upon our evil
zombie nerds!"

# CHAPTER 19

# THE BIG SWITCHEROO

Klax returned with a carton of SUPER EVIL RAPID-GROWTH JUICE, and placed it on the control panel.

"*Soon*," said Jennifer, "Earth will be *OURS*!"

The three aliens threw back their heads and laughed and laughed.

Suddenly, George got an idea.

He whispered to Harold for a second or two, then he quietly reached through the bars of the jail cell and swiped Klax's carton of SUPER EVIL RAPID-GROWTH JUICE.

George carefully peeled the label off the carton, and stuck it over the label of his ULTRA NASTY SELF-DESTRUCT JUICE.

While he was busy doing that, Harold reached through the bars and switched the labels of the spray gun and the fuel tank.

Finally, George reached back through the bars and put his carton of ULTRA NASTY SELF-DESTRUCT JUICE (which now read SUPER EVIL RAPID-GROWTH JUICE) on the control panel.

"I don't get it," whispered Captain Underpants. "The fuel tank now says SPRAY GUN, and the spray gun now says FUEL TANK, and the rapid-growth juice has been replaced with self-destruct juice. . . What's it all mean?"

"You'll find out," said Harold, sadly.

When the three evil space guys had finished laughing triumphantly, Jennifer reached for the carton that read SUPER EVIL RAPID-GROWTH JUICE and poured it into the nozzle that read SPRAY GUN.

"Oh, I get it," said Captain Underpants. "That space guy didn't pour growth juice into the spray gun – he poured self-destruct juice into the *fuel tank*!"

"Yep," George said sadly.

"And that means this spaceship thingy is going to explode into millions of pieces!"

"Right," said Harold gloomily.

The spaceship began to sputter and shake as smoke billowed out of the control panels. Soon sparks were flying and ceiling tiles were falling.

Captain Underpants smiled proudly because he had figured out George's plan. But his smile didn't last long.

"Hey," he cried. "*WE'RE* in the space-ship thingy! What's gonna happen to *us*?"

"We had to sacrifice ourselves to save the world," said George. "I'm afraid we're not going to make it."

"*Of course* we'll make it," cried Captain Underpants. "We've got *Wedgie Power* on our side!"

# CHAPTER 20
## THE GREAT ESCAPE

Captain Underpants grabbed a roll of toilet paper from the jail cell lavatory.

"We can swing to safety on *this*!" he said.

"You can't *swing* on toilet paper," said Harold.

"Sure I can," said Captain Underpants. "I just did it in my last comic book!"

Captain Underpants opened the jail cell
window and tossed the toilet paper into a
tall tree below them. "Come on, fellas," he
said. "Let's swing out of here before this
spaceship explodes!"

"That toilet paper won't hold you," said
George. "It's not strong enough!"

"Sure it is," said Captain Underpants.
"It's *two-ply*!"

George and Harold grabbed Captain Underpants's cape. "Don't jump!" they cried.

But Captain Underpants wouldn't listen. He jumped out the window with George and Harold still clinging to his cape.

"AAAAAAAAAAAAAAAHGH!" they screamed as they fell to the ground and were killed instantly.

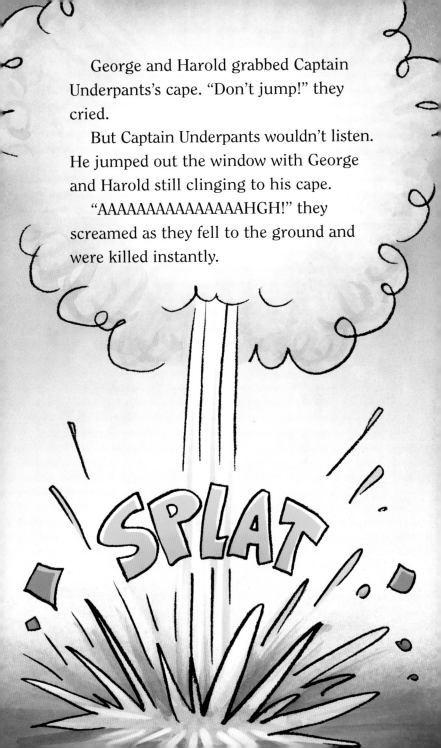

Just kidding.

Of course, the toilet paper could not support the weight of our three heroes, and for a moment, it looked like they were doomed.

But suddenly, Captain Underpants's red polyester cape opened up like a parachute— *PHOOOOP!*

George, Harold and the Waistband Warrior floated down safely as the spaceship above them exploded.

### KA-BOOM!

"Hallelujah!" cried Harold. *"We're not gonna die!* WE'RE NOT GONNA DIE!"

"Or. . ." said George. "Maybe we *are*."

# CHAPTER 21
# THE DELIRIOUSLY DANGEROUS DEATH-DEFYING DANDELION OF DOOM

George, Harold and Captain Underpants floated downwards, directly into the waiting jaws of the Dandelion of Doom.

"Aw, *man!*" cried Harold. "We *could* have got killed in a cool exploding spaceship. But instead, we're gonna get eaten by a *dandelion*. How *humiliating!*"

"Yeah," George moaned. "People are going to be giggling at our funerals."

The dandelion munched Captain Underpants and swung George and Harold around like a couple of rag dolls.

The two boys flew off and landed on the roof of the school.

"HELP MEEEeeEEEEeeEEEeeeEEE," screamed Captain Underpants as the Dandelion of Doom swung him back and forth.

"What should we do?" cried Harold.

"I've got an idea," said George. "It's a
bad idea, and I know we're going to regret
it, but we've got to act fast! The fate of the
entire planet is in our hands."

The next time the giant evil dandelion lurched towards the boys, George poured some EXTRA-STRENGTH SUPER POWER JUICE into Captain Underpants's mouth.

"What do you think is going to happen now?" asked Harold.

"I don't know," said George. "But I have a feeling it's gonna involve incredibly graphic violence!"

# CHAPTER 22
# THE INCREDIBLY GRAPHIC VIOLENCE CHAPTER, PART 2 (IN FLIP-O-RAMA™)

# WARNING:

The following chapter contains **scenes of a very unpleasant nature.**

All nastiness was performed by a qualified stuntman and a licensed stuntplant. Do not attempt to battle giant evil dandelions at home, even if you have recently consumed Extra-Strength Super Power Juice.

Such behaviour could result in serious boo-boos.

—The National Board of Boo-Boo Prevention

# FLIP-O-RAMA 4

(pages 117 and 119)

Remember, flip *only* page 117.
While you are flipping, be sure you
can see the picture on page 117
*and* the one on page 119.
If you flip quickly, the two
pictures will start to look like
<u>one</u> *animated* picture.

Don't forget to
add your own sound-effects!

LEFT HAND HERE

# WHEN DANDELIONS ATTACK

117

RIGHT
THUMB
HERE

RIGHT
INDEX
FINGER
HERE

118

# WHEN DANDELIONS
# ATTACK

# FLIP-O-RAMA 5

(pages 121 and 123)

Remember, flip *only* page 121.
While you are flipping, be sure you
can see the picture on page 121
*and* the one on page 123.
If you flip quickly, the two
pictures will start to look like
<u>one</u> *animated* picture.

Don't forget to
add your own sound-effects!

LEFT HAND HERE

# THE WEDGIE
# WEED WHACKER

RIGHT
THUMB
HERE

# THE WEDGIE
# WEED WHACKER

123

# FLIP-O-RAMA 6

(pages 125 and 127)

Remember, flip *only* page 125.
While you are flipping, be sure you
can see the picture on page 125
*and* the one on page 127.
If you flip quickly, the two
pictures will start to look like
<u>one</u> *animated* picture.

Don't forget to
add your own sound-effects!

LEFT HAND HERE

HOORAY FOR
CAPTAIN
UNDERPANTS!

RIGHT
THUMB
HERE

126

# HOORAY FOR CAPTAIN UNDERPANTS!

# CHAPTER 23
# THE TWENTY-THIRD CHAPTER

Captain Underpants (with the help of his newly developed super powers) had defeated the deliriously dangerous death-defying Dandelion of Doom! Now, the only thing left to do was to stop the evil zombie nerds.

"Oh, *HOW* are we going to conquer the evil zombie nerds?" asked George. "How will we ever change them back to normal?"

"Well, we could try this ANTI-EVIL
ZOMBIE NERD JUICE," said Harold.

George rolled his eyes. "I was hoping
for something a *little* more dramatic,"
he said, "but we're running out of pages.
Let's do it."

So Harold mixed up a batch of ANTI-EVIL ZOMBIE NERD ROOT BEER, and ordered everybody in the school to drink some.

The evil zombie nerds lined up. "Must drink root beer," they moaned. "Must drink root beer."

When the last zombie nerd had swallowed his last sip of root beer, George ordered Captain Underpants to get dressed back up like Mr Krupp.

"But I'll lose my super powers if I put on clothing," said Captain Underpants. "The power of underwear must be—"

"Just put the clothes on, bub!" George instructed.

Captain Underpants did as he was told,
and then George poured water over the
hero's head.

"Now all we can do is wait," said
Harold. "Wait and hope that everybody
returns to normal."

# CHAPTER 24
# TO MAKE A LONG
# STORY SHORT

They did.

# CHAPTER 25
## BACK TO NORMAL?

"Hooray," said Harold. "It's great to have everybody back to normal."

"Yep," said George. "That's for sure."

But "back to normal" probably wasn't the best choice of words. For while the students and faculty were the same as they'd always been, something had definitely *changed* about Mr Krupp.

Because from that day on, whenever he heard the sounds of fingers snapping . . .

*SNAP!*

. . . Mr Krupp not only turned back into "you-know-who", but he also had *Extra-Strength Super Powers*.

And if you thought it was hard for George and Harold to keep up with him *before*, well. . .

. . .you ain't seen nothin' yet!

"OH, NO!" screamed Harold.

"HERE WE GO AGAIN!" screamed George.

Tree
HOUSE
COMIX
INC.
Presents

# DoG MaN

### and The wrath of Petey

AKshiN

Drama

Laffs

a epic novella by
George Beard and
Harold Hutchins

DOG man was the Best cop of the world.

we LOVE you DOG man.

But He Had one weakni-ss.

Trash

Hey DOG man, Quit eating out of that Garbage can!

munch munch

and Quit rolling in that dead Fish!

POLIS cheef

and Quit snif-ing that other DOGS Butt!

snif snif

POLIS cheef

3

4

5

6

meenwhile DOG man was Hiding in a alley

munch munch

Trash can

Then...

NEWS ★

PeTey Runs amuk

BuT where is DOG man huh?

Trash can

DOG man Felt ashamed.

He knew he Must Be Brave

So DOG man Returned BRAVISHLY To Save the Day

7

Dog Man serched for Petey

Soon He Picked up a trale.

snif snif

It Leaded strate to Peteys Hideout.

snif snif snif

Petey the worlds most evilest cat

But it was a trap

gess what?

ITS Bath Time

spray

8

# DOG man GoT ascared!

# He digged a hole to get away

# Dog man Digged and digged

# But petey FOLOWED Him down the HOLE

DOG Man DUGGed all the way under the Zoo.

nks    HiPPO    LYen    eLiFent

He came up in the skunk cage.

ssss    sssss

Bathtime
for
Dog man

RIGHT
Thum
Here

Bathtime
for
Dog man

# FUN FACTS

### FUN FACT #1

Dav Pilkey never ate cafeteria food as a kid. He went to small church schools that didn't have lunch programmes, so he carried his lunch in a super-cool *Planet of the Apes* metal lunch box. Dav got his first taste of cafeteria food when he became a writer and began visiting elementary schools. Sometimes the food tasted OK, and other times it was pretty nasty, but it always smelled the same: kind of a combination of hamburger grease, diapers and musty beach towels, with just a slight whiff of burned plastic. He began to wonder what made the food smell that way. What if it was some sort of alien plot to control the brains of children? This idea was his inspiration for the third Captain Underpants book.

### FUN FACT #2

Xleqxisfp trees are over 700 feet tall and smell like raisin bread (though they taste kinda like chicken).

### FUN FACT #3

Dav no longer thinks that cafeteria food is an alien conspiracy to control the minds of children. Now he thinks it's a government conspiracy.

# HAVE YOU READ YOUR UNDERPANTS TODAY?

# ABOUT THE AUTHOR

When Dav Pilkey was a kid, his teachers thought he was disruptive, "behaviourally challenged", and in serious need of a major attitude adjustment.

When Dav wasn't writing sentences in the detention room, he could usually be found sitting at his private desk out in the hallway. There he spent his time writing and drawing his own original comic books about a superhero named Captain Underpants.